CHARMING THE DRAGON

KENZIE SKYE

CHAPTER
ONE

Macy

"I'm sorry about this, girl. We're just following orders," the hulking guard to my left of me says.

"Yeah, you heard what the oracle said," the other one chimes in from my right. Yeah, I heard what the oracle said, and I'd like to rip the bitch's eyes and hair out.

I'm sandwiched in between the huge men, each of them holding onto one of my arms like they're afraid I'm going to make a run for it. They don't need to worry about that, though. I understand my responsibility to the village, and I wouldn't try to shirk my duty that way.

I took my fate with dignity. I didn't break down and cry and make a commotion when the oracle announced that I was the virgin who was going to be sacrificed to the dragon up on Fire Mountain.

Yeah, not only is it bad enough that I'm the unlucky girl who gets to be sacrificed to the fearsome, fire-breathing dragon, but that oracle just outed me in front of the whole town for being a virgin. That's not really something I wanted the entire village to know, but I guess it won't matter whenever I become dragon food.

I don't exactly know what's going to happen up on the mountain, but that's what I assume it's going to be anyway.

Legend has it that no virgin has ever come down from the mountain after being taken up. Of course, that can't really be confirmed since one is only sent up every one hundred years.

Lucky me that I would be alive on the centennial that a new one is chosen. And with my shitty luck, I would be the one chosen.

I'd be lying if I said I wasn't a little scared, but what concerns me the most isn't my own fate. If

I'm going to be eaten by a dragon, no amount of moping and whining about it is going to change it. No, what worries me the most is who's going to take care of my little sister now that I'm gone?

I just turned eighteen, but my sister is only fourteen. Both of our parents died of the fever a couple of years ago, so it's just the two of us. I can't stand the thought of some old pervert getting his hands on her, but I know that with me out of the picture, marrying early is going to be about the only thing that will save her.

The irony of the situation isn't lost on me. I'm wearing a gorgeous dress of light, peachy pink that flows all the way down to my ankles. It's strapless and held up by my petite bosom. My honey-colored hair was brushed until it shone and left to cascade freely down my shoulders.

It's like the townsfolk wanted to make sure I looked really pretty for my funeral. Maybe dragons only want to eat pretty things. I don't know.

I look up at the fiery mountain top. I can't help but think that Fire Mountain is aptly named. The closer we get to the top of the mountain, the hotter it gets, which is just the opposite of how it usually is. It's usually colder on mountaintops, but not up here on Fire Mountain. I guess it's the dragon. He must generate so much heat that it keeps it warmer up here.

I don't know which death would be more preferable—combusting to death from the heat or being eaten alive by an enormous dragon.

I guess I'll find out soon enough because we're almost at the top.

When we reach the mouth of the cave, I can feel the two men trembling from where they each grip my arms. I have to suppress a wry grin. Shouldn't *I* be the one trembling? What are they so scared for? They get to go back home to their families. I'm the one being left up here with the dragon.

They deposit me at the mouth of the cave and then shuffle their feet like the cowards they are, casting me pitying, sorrowful glances. "We're real sorry about this, girl," they tell me. To their credit, they truly do seem to mean their words.

"Macy," I tell them.

They blink and look at me questioningly.

"My name is Macy," I elaborate. "I figure it would be kind of sad for the last people I see to not even know my name, so there it is."

The men stare at me in horror, and neither

offers to tell me his name. I guess they figure what's the point.

Oh well.

I take pity on them and don't make it too hard on them. I know they're just following orders and that it would have been their necks too if they hadn't agreed to drag me up here. Not that they'd had to drag me. I came readily enough, but still.

I wave my hand at them cheerily, "Oh, perk up boys. Don't worry about me. I'll be fine."

They cast dubious glances at one another. "Are you sure you're alright, girl?" one of them asks me, obviously thinking that I've already gone mad. I notice he doesn't speak my name, but that's okay.

My smile only widens. "Of course. Why wouldn't I be? I'm happy to be sacrificed for my village!" I make my voice bright and cheery.

The two befuddled men share another glance with one another. They obviously don't feel good about leaving me in this state, which is ironic because would they feel better if I were in hysterics, sobbing and kicking and screaming? Something tells me they would, that my positive attitude is worse for them than the alternative. I guess because it's not predictable, and men don't like a woman who's not predictable or who doesn't fit their mold.

On second thought, it's probably for the best that I'm the one being sacrificed to a dragon because I never would have fit the mold of the perfect housewife that would have been expected of me had I stayed in the village. I suppose, all things considered, this does work out the way it should. I still want to strangle that oracle, though.

I smile before I clap my hands together in excitement. "Now where's this fire-breathing dragon I'm supposed to meet?"

"Right here," a booming voice thunders.

Macy

I can't help the startled jump I give at the unexpected voice. I see both of the guards' eyes go wide before they scramble down the mountain without another word to me. So much for feeling sorry about leaving me up here.

I smile dryly as I turn around and cross my arms at the humongous beast in front of me. My head cranes up at the way he towers over me. He's covered in red scales. My eyes trail over his wide-spread wings all the way down to his clawed feet. I gulp as I stare at him. My god, he's magnificent.

He's easily the most beautiful creature I've ever seen. I'm so in awe of him I forget my fear.

Part of what amazes me most is the way his wings become so dark a red where they extend from his back that they almost look to be a deep purple. He steps out of the mouth of the cave into the sunlight, and his scales twinkle and glimmer like they're studied with a thousand tiny diamonds. It's the most mesmerizing sight I've ever seen.

His amber eyes meet mine. They're so bright, they seem to glow with a fire on their own. The intensity with which they stare at me should scare me, but it sends a tingle racing down my spine.

The dragon frowns before he notes, "You're not scared of me?"

I shake my head. "No. Well," I backtrack, "I mean, yes, you are quite fearsome, but I was momentarily so blinded by your beauty that I couldn't focus on my fear."

The dragon blinks and looks taken aback.

"Of course, I'm also shocked that you can talk because in all the legends I've ever heard of virgins being sacrificed to the dragon on the mountain, no one ever told me you could talk. They certainly never mentioned it in preparation today."

"Preparation?" He raises a questioning eyebrow at me.

"Oh yes." I nod my head. "They groomed me and put me in this silly little dress and told me the importance of doing my duty after the oracle picked me to be the unlucky one to be sacrificed to you. No offense."

He regards me curiously, as if he doesn't know what to make of me. I guess I can't really blame him there. I don't know what to make of myself. Maybe I have gone into a form of temporary insanity because he's right. I should exhibit fear, yet instead I'm just intrigued.

Dragons can talk! That knowledge is thrilling, and I suddenly have a million questions I want to ask him. Plus, I remind myself, if I can keep him entertained and keep him talking, then maybe that'll give him a reason not to eat me—at least not right away.

"You are a..." he speaks slowly, as if he's searching for the right work before he ends with, "a curious creature."

"Funny, I was just thinking the same thing about you." I smile at him brightly.

"You are not what I expected in a sacrifice."

I cock my head to the side and ask him, "Am I

so different from the other sacrifices you received?"

The dragon takes a step back and spreads his wings before he draws them closer about his body again, in what I can only ascribe to as a stretch. "I wouldn't know," he admits. "I've never had any other sacrifices."

I blink at that knowledge. "But my village sacrifices a virgin to the dragon on this mountain every year. At least that's what they say."

"They might do it," the dragon admits, "but I've never received one before because I am new to this mountaintop."

I blink. "Oh, so is there a new dragon every year?"

The dragon flicks his tail. "I can't answer that. All I know is that I was sent here this year."

"Why? What happened to the previous dragon?"

His nostrils flare as if he's already tired of my thousand questions. "That is not your concern," he snaps.

"So, you do know and you just don't want to tell me?" I press, my curiosity getting the better of me. It's probably not wise for me to goad the creature that holds my life in his claws, but really, what do I have to lose at this point? Being on the brink of death apparently makes me stupidly brave.

The dragon looks heavenward before his eyes land on me again. "Are you always this chatty?"

I shrug. "I don't know. It's just fascinating to me being in the presence of a dragon and knowing that he can eat me at any moment."

The dragon blinks and takes a step back. "Eat you?"

"Yes. Isn't that what dragons do with their sacrifices? No virgin has ever come off the mountaintop after being sent up, so we naturally assume that the dragons devour them."

The dragon looks heavenward again in a gesture that's reminiscent of rolling his eyes. "I am not going to eat you, child."

Hope takes flight in my chest. "You're not? So, are you going to let me go?"

He frowns. "I'm afraid I can't do that either, but rest assured, you won't be eaten."

"Oh," I brighten. "Well, that's wonderful news. In fact, that's the best news I've received all day." I laugh, and he looks at me like I've lost the last marble I had in my head. Maybe I have. I don't know. I don't know the first thing about how to navigate a situation like this. First, I found out I was going to be sacrificed to a dragon. I was fully expecting to be eaten, and now I come up here and said dragon is, in fact, not going to eat me. It's been one hell of a day.

"So, what are you going to do with me?" I ask him.

He studies me, his amber eyes never leaving me as they pass up and down my frame.

I feel another one of those tingles of awareness go up my spine, and then I consider the way the townsfolk primped and prodded me, making me look more beautiful than I ever have.

"Oh, no," I shake my head as I take a step back from him. "No way, buster. Don't even think about it." I said I would do my duty to the village. I was willing to be sacrificed as in eaten—hopefully in one painless bite—but to be torn apart by some big dragon dick. No way. That is not what I signed up for. "Just eat me instead."

CHAPTER

THREE

Blaine

I look at the curious little human in front of me in confusion. "Eat you instead? My god, child, what do you think I'm going to do to you?"

She's still shaking her head and backing away from me, edging closer toward the mouth of the cave.

A warning growl rumbles up from my throat without conscious thought. I don't like her getting too close to the mouth of the cave.

"Look, lover boy," she points a shaky finger at me. "I'm not your mate or some sick shit like that, so if you think you're going to kill me with your humongous dragon dick, you can just keep moving. I would rather throw myself off this mountain top than be torn apart by some monster dick. No offense, but just look at you, and look at me. We are two puzzle pieces that don't fit together."

My eyes widen at both her candor and the visual she's presented. "No," I snort at her. "Calm down, child. That is *not* what I intend to do with you either."

Her shoulders only relax a bit before she shoots me a suspicious book. "You sure? Why did I have to be primped and prettied up to come up here?"

My nostrils flare as I take in her tiny form again. She certainly was primped and prettied. She's wearing a peachy pink dress that flows down to her feet. It shows off her shoulders and the pale column of her throat. She's so tiny and delicate-looking with her creamy skin and long honey-colored locks that hang down nearly to her waist. She has deep brown eyes set in a little heart-shaped face. Puffy pink lips and rosy cheeks give her a cherubic look.

"Fuck if I know," I growl out. "Who knows why

you villagers do anything you do?"

"So, if you're not going to eat me, and you don't want to, you know," she says as she gives me a pointed look, "then why was I sent up here?"

I glare at her. "Obviously to irritate the fuck out of me," I mumble to myself. This little thing hasn't stopped talking since she opened that pretty mouth of hers.

"What?" she asks, blinking at me innocently.

"Your guess is as good as mine," I speak loud enough so she can hear me now. "I'm new to this too, and there was nothing in the handbook that told me what to do or expect. All I know is that I can't let you go."

"How do you know that if no one told you what to do or expect?"

I pause, surprised by her astute observation. I answer honestly, "I don't know. It's just something in my instincts. I can't let you go. You were given to me, and you're mine now." I can't help the possessive rumble that accompanies my words when I tell her she's mine.

And it suddenly clicks within me. She *is* mine. I suddenly know that I value her above any of the treasures in my hoard. I don't know why.

"What's your name?" she suddenly asks me.

I'm completely taken aback. "No one has asked me my name for at least five centuries."

"I'm Macy." She offers me her name and then stands there blinking and waiting patiently for me to divulge my own.

"If I'm going to be here with you for the foreseeable future, don't you think that I should have something to call you rather than just "dragon," which seems kind of species-ist?"

"Species-ist?" I ask her.

"Yeah, it's kind of like racist, but for species."

I stare at her. "You're completely unlike any human I've ever met."

She smiles at me. It's a pretty smile, one that could rival the brightness of the morning sun. I find that I quite enjoy seeing it.

"I'll take that as a compliment since most humans are shitty," she says brightly.

I shake my head, a chuckle rumbling up out of my chest despite myself.

"Blaine," I finally tell her.

"Blaine," she echoes my name, and I rumble in satisfaction. Something in my chest tightens. I love the way my name sounds coming from her lips, or maybe it's just that I haven't heard my name spoken aloud by any other living organism for so long.

I watch in amazement as she takes a few more steps over to me before she sits on a rock near my head and looks up at me. "So, what do you do up here all day on Fire Mountain?"

I glance down at her. Is she serious? I still can't get over the fact that this little human isn't afraid of me.

"You do realize I breathe fire?" I ask her.

She shrugs one delicate shoulder. "So, is that like a hobby or something?" She blinks up at me as comprehension dawns on her face. "Oh, you're still wondering why I'm not running in fright from you. Well, I'll tell you, Blaine. You already told me you're not going to eat me or try to mate me or something, but you, unfortunately, won't be able to let me go, so I figure we might as well make the most of this situation, don't you?"

I stare at her for a beat, still not sure what to make of her.

"I sit here and enjoy being left alone," I finally grumble at her.

She doesn't seem to be offended by my surly tone at all. No, she merely chirps, "Well, that's no fun at all. We'll have to find some fun things to do now that I'm here."

"Fun?" I ask her, not familiar with the concept.

"Yeah, fun, you know, things that you do just for enjoyment. Like we could talk or play games or travel."

"We can't travel." I immediately shut that idea down. "I have to stay here and guard my hoard."

She blinks before she looks behind me to my many jewels and treasures. "Oh yeah, I forgot how greedy you dragons are."

"Greedy?" I growl in outrage.

"Yeah, you love shiny things and can't even live your life for guarding them."

I can't help the growl that rumbles of out of me.

"Oh, I'm not judging you," she goes on, "so don't get all upset. I'm just saying I forgot how dragons were like that."

"Considering how you didn't even know we could talk, I would hardly call you an authority on our species." I point out dryly.

"Good point," she immediately concedes, "so why don't you tell me everything there is to know about your kind? You know, since I'm going to be living with you now, I need to know more about your species."

I close my eyes for a beat. For the love of all that's shiny, does this little human ever shut up?

Instead of answering, I tell her, "It's late, and I'm sure your journey up here was tiring. Let me get you something to eat, and then you should rest."

Before she can say anything, I take off flying from the cave. I circle around and hover right in front of the mouth where she's staring at me with wide eyes. I flap my wings. "Oh, and Macy. Don't even try to escape while I'm gone because if you do, I will hunt you down, and I will find you, and while I said I wouldn't eat you or rape you, I never said I wouldn't punish you if you disobey me."

Her eyes are still wide, her mouth parted when I turn and begin scoping the land, looking for something to feed my tiny human.

As befuddling and chatty as she is, I can't deny that my heart thrills a bit at having something of my very own to take care of—like a pet but more than that.

It's like I suddenly have a new reason for living.

Macy

When Blaine comes back, he has a rabbit carcass gripped in his front right claw. He drops it unceremoniously in front of me before looking at me expectantly.

I glance down at the carcass before looking up at him in confusion.

"Well, don't humans eat this?" His amber eyes glow at me with pride.

I pick the carcass up gingerly. I guess it's a good thing my dad taught me how to skin an animal before he died.

"Sure, yeah, thanks," I tell him, not wanting to seem ungrateful. "I can work with this. Do you have a knife?"

"What for?" Blaine asks me.

"So I can skin the rabbit and cook it."

"What's wrong with it the way it is?" Blaine asks me.

I raise an eyebrow at him as I wrinkle my nose at his implication. "It's raw."

"Ah, yes. I forgot you humans prefer not to consume raw meat."

"Yes, that's right." I nod in relief when Blaine doesn't seem to be offended. Instead, he stalks over to his treasure hoard and rifles through it before he pushes a dagger over at me.

"Will this work?" he asks me.

My jaw drops open when I pick up the jewel-encrusted dagger. The emeralds and rubies embedded in its hilt glint in the warm lighting of the cave.

"Um, yeah. This'll do."

Blaine tracks my every movement as I skin the rabbit and cut it into pieces. He motions to a bowl of water sitting in the cave's corner. I don't even ask him how it got there. I know he didn't go draw the water from anywhere, but when my eyes trail up along the top of the cave, I see he's ingeniously got the bowl sitting where fresh water drips in from the top of the cave. I don't know what dragons need water for. Do they drink water like other species, or will the water quench the fire in their bellies?

I almost giggle at my silly thoughts, but I don't want to offend Blaine by asking him, so I refrain.

After I wash my hands, I return to the raw meat.

Blaine pulls his feet up under him as he sits next to me and looks at me expectantly. "Okay, now what?" He watches me as if he's a student trying to learn how to cook.

"I need a fire to cook it over."

"Stand back," Blaine warns me before he breathes a puff a fire on the ground before us.

I stare in amazement at the strong, roaring fire that takes root.

"Wow," I breathe, "You'd definitely be helpful to have around in a pinch." I say as I watch the flames jump.

"What?" Blaine looks at me curiously.

I shake my head. "Nevermind."

Blaine tracks my every movement as I help myself to items from his hoard. I use a sword as a skewer to roast the meat, and then I help myself to a gold, diamond-encrusted plate to place the cooked meat on to cool.

Blaine doesn't protest me using any of his things. No, if I'm not mistaken, his eyes seem to glow with warmth at seeing me use them.

He watches me eat the rabbit, shaking his head to decline when I offer him a bite. I was hungrier than I thought I was and eat nearly the entire thing.

"Do you eat humans?" I ask him.

Blaine chuckles before he answers, "No, I don't."

"Do any dragons?"

Blaine makes a movement that I can only imagine is a dragon shrug. "If they do, it's to send a message. Humans aren't part of a typical dragon diet." Blaine's eyes slide over to me before he adds, "Contrary to what you humans like to believe."

"What do you eat then?"

"We're carnivorous, so any manner of beast, really, though I prefer bear and moose."

I try not to wrinkle my nose in distaste, but I must fail because Blaine chuckles again.

"Did you eat before you came back?" I ask him.

"Yes," he answers simply.

"I take it you don't, uh, cook your food."

All of Blaine's teeth show as he smiles at me. "No, not unless you count breathing fire on them prior to consuming them."

I swallow, as I'm reminded of just what kind of dangerous creature Blaine is. I don't know if consuming food has suddenly cured me of my previous nonchalance, but now I'm acutely aware that I have a fire-breathing dragon sitting in front of me.

As if he can sense my sudden wariness, Blaine adds, "I would never hurt you, Macy. You are my most-valued treasure now."

I blink at that, something in his tone giving me pause. "I am?" I ask incredulously.

"You are," Blaine's voice is smooth and almost seems to croon at me.

"I don't understand my purpose here," I finally state. "I thought I was supposed to be a sacrifice."

"Are you telling me you're disappointed I don't plan on eating you or otherwise killing you?"

My face blushes when I think of how Blaine could easily kill me with sex. Why the hell does my stomach do a little flip at the thought? He's a *dragon*. Humans and dragons don't mix. It's biologically impossible.

Still, for one horrifying moment, I wonder what it would be like if Blaine could have his way with me.

My face is blushing, and it doesn't go unnoticed by Blaine. The dragon is perceptive, if nothing else, and promptly asks me, "What are you thinking about?"

I don't answer him. Instead, I stretch and put on a yawn. "I'm tired. I guess that meal made me drowsy."

Blaine is quick to tell me, "Then you should get your rest. The eventful day you've had is probably catching up to you."

I nod, relaxing when he doesn't press me for an answer why I was blushing. I think I'd die if had to admit the turn my wayward thoughts had taken.

I look around the cave and frown when I don't see anywhere soft to sleep. "Where should I sleep?" I ask him.

He follows my gaze around the cave. "Where do humans usually like to sleep?"

"On something soft. Do you have some

bearskins or something lying around left over from one of your meals?" I joke.

"Unfortunately, no," Blaine tells me with a frown.

"That's okay. I'll made do on this rock." I try to lay down on the rock I've been sitting on. It's dreadfully uncomfortable, but hey, at least I'm alive and not eaten, so I should be thankful for anything.

I'm only laying on the uncomfortable rock for a moment before I feel myself being lifted into the air. I gasp, my hands flying down to wrap around the huge claw banded gently around my waist as Blaine picks me up.

"What are you—?"

Blaine cuts me off by shushing me. "Giving you a soft place to sleep."

He lays me on one of his arms in the crook of his neck, and I don't know what I expected a dragon's scales to feel like, but it's not the softness that meets me. I guess I expected a dragon to feel, well, *scaly*, but where Blaine lays me is squishy soft and not hard at all.

"Oh." My voice comes out breathy.

"How's that?" I feel the rumble of Blaine's voice as it vibrates throughout his entire body.

"Much better. Thank you," I whisper. "Are you sure you don't mind me sleeping on you like this?"

Blaine's chuckle runs throughout my entire body like a massage. "Your slight weight isn't too heavy for me, if that's what you're implying," he teases me.

"Well, thank you," I tell him genuinely again. He didn't have to accommodate me, yet here he is offering to let me sleep on him, of all places.

"It's my pleasure to take care of you," his voice rumbles again.

I don't speak for a while. I just savor the softness of laying on Blaine and doze in his warmth. The dragon's body generates enough heat that I don't need any blankets.

"Blaine?" I finally speak, looking at him through half-lidded eyes.

"Yes, my treasure?"

The moniker sends a rush of warmth pulsing through me. No one has ever called me endearments, and I like the sound of Blaine referring to me as his treasure, like I'm something precious to him. My heart swells and instead of telling him "goodnight" like I intended, I hear myself admitting, "I'm glad you're the dragon I was sacrificed to."

He's quiet for a moment, but when he speaks, his voice sounds deeper than before. "Me too. Now, sleep, little one."

As if all I needed was his permission, I fall into a deep sleep—perhaps the most peaceful sleep I've ever had in my entire life.

CHAPTER

FIVE

Macy

I meant what I said before. I still don't fully understand my purpose for being here, but I guess that's not my place to understand. What I do know deep down in my soul is that Blaine won't hurt me. He's telling the truth when he tells me I'm his most treasured possession.

While the feminist in me might balk at being regarded as a possession, with a dragon, being a treasured possession is much more favorable to being food. If I'm being totally honest, it's not bad at all staying here with Blaine.

In fact, the dragon dotes on me. All I have to do is express a mild interest in something, and if he can get it for me, he does. I don't know where he gets the stuff he does, but every day he brings me clothing, books, and other amusements. He always carries them in a big sack, gripped in between his claws.

I'm still shocked that the dragon I thought would be my downfall has actually become my fierce protector and friend. If I wander too close to the mouth of the cave, his tail snakes around me, gently pulling me back. His amber eyes are always watching every movement I make. Instead of being unsettling, it's surprisingly comforting.

Blaine doesn't know his exact age, but he's many centuries old. I love to lie in my spot in the crook of his neck and feel the rumble of his voice as he speaks lowly to me. He recounts all the many things he's seen throughout his life. He's seen kingdoms come and go—ones that I've never even heard of because there're so ancient history didn't record them.

Blaine is like a huge encyclopedia. Any question I ask him he has an answer for. My dragon is highly intelligent. Yes, I've come to think of him as *my* dragon, claiming him as much as he's claimed me as his possession.

I figure if my fate is to be a sacrifice and live out the rest of my days up on this mountain, I got pretty lucky because the dragon I got as company is actually enjoyable. And he spoils me like I'm a pampered pet, and maybe that's how he sees me—as a pet, like a cute little kitten. That's honestly okay with me if it means his amber eyes will glow at me like that and I get to hear his deep chuckles and molten voice every day.

Contrary to what people make them out to be like, dragons aren't horrible creatures—at least mine isn't. He's thoughtful and kind and funny and beautiful. God, he's so beautiful. I could stare at him in awe all day. I especially love it when he steps into the sunlight and I can see his scales glitter.

His scales aren't just one uniform red. No, they consist of various hues. Some currant, some cherry, some crimson, some ruby, and some even a beautiful berry color. The way that red blends and tapers off into a plum and then a rich amethyst near his back is mesmerizing.

As the days go by, we grow even closer in our

friendship, and I wonder how I ever got along without Blaine. He's such a part of my life now, embedded deep into my heart—so much so that when I fall asleep, I dream of him in my dreams.

In my dreams, he's not a dragon. He's a man, a gorgeously handsome man. I wake up confused, my body wet and aching, and then reality comes crashing down on me when I realize Blaine is in fact not a man. He's a dragon, and it could never work between us romantically.

It's ironic too because Blaine is the perfect man—only he's not a man, and it's such a shame because he's attentive and kind and witty and funny and smart. I love being around him. I'm comfortable with him.

It startles me when I realize Blaine would make a perfect husband.

Except for the tiny fact that he's a fire-breathing dragon.

Yeah, except for that.

~

Blaine

I am in love with Macy. Everything about my little human fascinates me. The solitude that I once thought I savored is gone. In its place is her sweet chatter, and while I might joke that it irritates me, I don't think I can live without it now. In fact, I wonder how I did live without it for so long. She brings light to my dreary existence. I love everything about her—from her honey-colored locks to the tips of her tiny little feet.

I watch her all day as she looks around my cave. I let her use any of my treasures she desires, and every time I go out, I bring her back little gifts and trinkets. She's crafted a sort of room in the corner out of expensive fabrics hanging up on golden spikes. She has enough fabrics now that she has a small bed area set up, but she still sleeps in the crook of my neck every night. I'm pleased that she hasn't insisted on sleeping in the bedding she's gathered over in that corner. I enjoy feeling her tiny weight on me too much.

I find out more about what she likes to eat. Humans aren't carnivorous like us dragons, so I bring her fruits and vegetables and other foods that she can eat besides meat. She seems to prefer those to meat, actually.

As hard as it is to believe, I think my little human likes me, too. She's always asking me questions and then staring at me in wide-eyed wonder when I can provide her with the answers. I have to confess it gives me a heady rush to see her looking at me with such hero worship in her eyes.

By all rights, she should fear me, yet she doesn't. I think she can sense deep down that I would truly never hurt her. Plus, I've told her so frequently, assuring her she is my most valued treasure. I haven't told her this, but I would give up my entire hoard for her. None of the gold or jewels in my stash compare to her. I've never had anything like her, and I guard her possessively, my eyes trailing her everywhere she goes. If she finds my constant attention unsettling, she doesn't show it.

Like her, I still don't understand her purpose for being here or mine for being sent here. All I know is that when the goddess told me I had to move to this mountaintop, it was an order I couldn't disobey—just like I suppose Macy couldn't disobey her village when they insisted on sacrificing her to me.

Despite the events that brought us together, I

am glad for them because my life is filled with more joy and meaning than I ever thought it could be. I don't know what the other dragons did with their sacrifices, but I know I will treasure mine always.

I watch over her now as she lays sleeping on me. The little rise and fall of her chest comforts me. I like the way her hair splays on my scales and the way her little pink lips part softly in her slumber. She's like a sleeping angel, and my chest squeezes.

It makes no sense. I don't just love her. I'm *in love* with her and with that comes all the feelings that come with being in love with another creature. It doesn't matter that I'm a dragon and she's a human and that I can never claim her physically the way I long to do so. I can't stop the way my heart beats for her or this obsession I have with her.

And I can't help thinking that fate is a cruel bitch for making the female I fall in love with be such a different species from me. I wish she were a dragon or me a man. I don't really care which. I just wish we were the same enough for me to show her just how much I love her. She's completely charmed me, but it can never be, so I must content myself with her companionship. That is enough. It's certainly more than I ever expected for my wretched existence.

CHAPTER

SIX

Macy

I've gotten so used to having Blaine around that I hate it when he leaves. I realize he's going out to get provisions for me, but I get lonely—even if he's only gone for half a day.

I usually don't wander too close to the mouth of the cave because I can see how much it worries him when I do. But he's not here, and I'm strangely becoming kind of claustrophobic without him. It doesn't really make sense. I know you would think I would be more claustrophobic with a ginormous dragon taking up a huge amount of space in the cave, but I feel more strangled in here all alone.

I step up to the mouth of the cave, turning my face up, closing my eyes to feel the sunlight warming my cheeks. There's a slight breeze blowing today, and it cools my skin. I look down over the landscape. It really is exquisite up here. I can see everything for miles. I think I see the village, and my heart pangs. It's not that I miss the village itself so much as my sister. I wonder how she's doing, if she's taking care of herself or she's been forced to get married. Lily is the only thing I miss.

I sigh as I gaze out over the landscape wistfully, wishing that there was some way I could make sure my sister's okay. I feel kind of guilty for finding contentment in my situation while she's out there all alone without me. I've been taking care of her for so long. I can only hope that she was able to find her own way without me.

A strong breeze suddenly blows, twining my skirt around my ankle. I take a step back from the edge with my arms outstretched about me for balance, but I trip on my swirling skirts. Panic seizes me as I go toppling over the edge, flapping my arms like they're suddenly wings that will take flight. Of course, I don't begin flying, so I go falling down, down.

It happens so fast. I close my eyes shut, bracing for the impact of whenever I eventually hit the ground. Hopefully, my death will be quick and merciful.

My expected death never comes, though, because suddenly I'm gripped in between claws, and I feel myself being lifted higher in the air.

I peek over my eyes and gasp whenever I see Blaine has me firmly yet gently clasped in his large claw. He carries me back onto the ledge before landing beside me and ushering me into the cave with that long tail of his.

I turn to him in relief, prepared to thank him for rescuing me, but my eyes widen when I see his eyes are glowing nearly red with fury.

"I wasn't trying to escape," I rush to tell him, assuming that's the only reason he could look so angry.

"Then what were you doing?" His voice is a booming growl that cracks like thunder. Smoke unfurls from his nostrils.

"Getting some sun," I tell him as I take an instinctive step away from him. I still don't believe Blaine would ever purposefully hurt me, but I've never seen him breathing smoke before either.

"You could have been hurt." His tone is still hard and angry.

I swallow. "I know that, but I wasn't. Thanks to you," I tell him gently.

He's still tense, and his eyes are still glowing red. His big chest puffs out, and he's almost vibrating with rage. I can hear the fire scratching against his voice when he bites out, "Do you know what I would do if something happened to you?"

"I just wanted some sunlight and fresh air," I whisper. "I get claustrophobic in this cave without you."

He blinks as he continues to stare at me, his chest heaving up and down before he finally calms. I watch him warily as his muscles slowly relax. "Of course. You're tired of the cave."

I nod at him. "It's not you," I rush to assure him. "You're wonderful company, and I've come to think of you as my closest friend."

"Friend," he echoes hollowly, a strange note in his voice.

I nod. "Yes, but I would still like to feel the sunlight on my skin from time to time and breathe in some fresh air."

"You should have told me sooner. But never venture past the mouth of this cave when I'm not here again. Do you understand?" His voice is stern, and while I would normally bristle at being spoken to in such a manner, I know he's only over-reacting out of concern for me. Actually, I have to admit that he might not be overreacting. He *did* come back to see me falling to my death. I can't imagine what a scare that must have given him.

I bite my lip and nod because I realize his concerns are valid. I was lucky today. If he hadn't shown up when he did, I would be mincemeat at the bottom of this mountain.

He walks over to me and then extends his head down to the floor. He looks up at me with his head at my feet. "Get on," he orders me with his glowing eyes still trained on me.

"What?" I ask him in confusion.

He makes a little motion with his head. "You want to go out? You want some sunlight and fresh air? I'll take you. Climb up on my back and hold on to my neck."

A thrill goes through me. He's going to let me ride him?

I've always wondered what it would be like to fly, but I never presumed to ask Blaine to let me ride him. I didn't know if that would be offensive.

Blaine nudges me, and I scramble atop him.

"Wrap your arms around my neck tight, and don't let go," he instructs me.

I do as he says. Then, with a sprint and a wide unfurling of his wings, we're off.

Blaine

My heart soars higher than my wings take us whenever my ears are met with Macy's delighted giggles. She's holding tightly about my neck just like I told her, but I requested for her to do that more for my enjoyment than her own safety. There's no way I'll ever drop her, and even if she did slide off of me, I would catch her. No doubt about that.

I'm internally cursing myself for never considering that my little treasure would want to leave the cave. I so easily forget that she's a creature of the sunlight. She must have found it stifling being holed up in a cave like a hermit—or a dragon.

A wry smile twists my lips as I take her all across the land, swooping low enough that she can see all the pretty flora and fauna. I don't swoop too near her village, though, because not only do I not want to scare the villagers, but I don't want to alarm them if they see Macy flying atop my back.

Humans are funny creatures, and they could start all kinds of rumors about Macy if they think she's acted out of the norm and charmed the dragon she was supposed to be sacrificed to. They might dub her a witch or some sort, and while it doesn't matter since she's going to stay with me from here on out. I don't want my treasure's reputation tarnished that way.

When we arrive back in the cave, Macy slides off me with a huge smile on her face. I grin back at her. "Did you enjoy that?"

"Very much so," she breathes out before she looks down, hiding her eyes from me.

I frown at the sudden change, instinctively knowing something is up. Macy never hides from me. From the moment I met her, she's always been blatantly honest. "What is it, Macy?"

"It's nothing." She shakes her head.

I growl, "It's not nothing. Tell me."

Something has upset her. She's still not happy, and I need to know what's going on.

She peaks a look up at me before she bites her lip and then lets out a little sigh. "I don't want to sound ungrateful because I am super grateful for how nice you've been and everything you've done, the amazing ride you just gave me..." she trails off.

"But?" I prompt her, sensing there's more.

"It's my sister," she finally admits. "I'm worried about her."

I blink. "I didn't know you have a sister."

She nods her head vigorously. "Yes, she's only fourteen years old, and I worry about how she's getting along now that I'm no longer there to watch over her."

My brow furrows. "Your parents—"

She interrupts me by shaking her head sadly. "They died a few years ago. It's just been me and Bree for a while now. Flying over the village reminded me of her."

She says softly before she adds, "Not that I don't think of her every day."

"You've never mentioned anything," I point out.

She looks at me helplessly. "What's the point? This is my fate. To be up on this mountain with you. You told me yourself you can't let me leave. There's no use in making us both feel bad for circumstances we can't change."

I look at my little treasure, my heart softening at the sincerity in her eyes. All this time she's been worried about her little sister, yet she didn't want to upset me or seem ungrateful, so she never brought it up.

I finally smile at her. She looks a bit taken aback by my grin, so I rush to assure her, "Oh, my precious child, if only you had mentioned this sooner."

She looks at me in confusion. "Why?"

Instead of answering, I stalk over to my hoard of treasures and rifle through it until I find what I'm looking for. I kick the little handheld mirror over to her.

She picks it up cautiously, giving me a questioning look as she does so. I nod at the mirror. "Gaze into it and think of your sister when you do so."

After giving me one last glance like she thinks

I'm crazy, she he turns her head down and does as I tell her. I know the moment the magic has worked because I hear her gasp. She touches the mirror reverently, stroking her finger over the glass gently. "Bree!" she exclaims with an amazed smile on her face as she watches her sister.

I smile at the joy I feel radiating from her.

"She's doing just fine," Macy finally tells me with a wide smile as she glances up at me. She lets out a little laugh before she adds, "She's gathering the eggs from the chicken coop. It looks like she's still living on her own. She hasn't been married off to the highest bidder." Macy's shoulders visibly slump in relief before she confesses, "That was my biggest worry, that they would force her to marry some old toad."

She watches the mirror for a while longer before she reluctantly hands it back. I shake my head. "Keep it. That way you can look at it whenever the longing for your sister gets to be too much."

Tears glisten in Macy's eyes, and her lip trembles. She doesn't speak. Instead, she turns around and pockets the mirror away in her little makeshift bed area over in the cave's corner before she walks back over to me and crawls up into her little place in the crook of my neck and wraps her arms around me.

And it could be my imagination, but I think I feel the tiny press of her lips against my scales.

For the millionth time, I wish I was a man and not what I am.

Blaine

Macy and I grow closer than ever after I give her the mirror that will allow her to see her sister. She's happier and lighter now that she knows her sister is okay. She gazes into the mirror often, but she hasn't let it become an obsession. She doesn't stare at it non-stop. She gives me plenty of attention, which pleases me to no end.

I take her out for a ride on my back every day that the weather permits. While I can fly in any weather, I refuse to take Macy out when it's raining or storming. I don't want to chance anything happening to her. Humans are such fragile creatures. I don't want her to get a cold and come down ill—especially since I'm not a human and wouldn't be able to properly care for her.

As luck would have it, though, Macy's sister comes down ill. I see the worry lining Macy's face whenever she looks in the mirror and sees her sister laid up in bed. Her sister's pallor is pale, and she clearly doesn't have any energy.

Macy has tears in her eyes when she looks up at me, her heart clearly breaking as she says in a shaky voice, "Blaine, she doesn't have anyone there to take care of her. It doesn't look like anyone even knows she's sick. What if she has a fever like my parents had?"

I try to assure her it's just a common cold and that she'll be okay, but as the days pass and her sister's health fails more, Macy becomes nearly inconsolable, and that makes me feel like the worst sort of predator for keeping her here.

Finally, I know what I must do, and it's with a heavy heart that I do it. I'll most assuredly die from this action, but I can't stand the thought of my little treasure upset, and she's obviously hurting over her sister.

I watch over Macy as she sleeps on me,

savoring the imprint of her on my skin. I'm trying to memorize every curve of her body and the sound of her gentle breathing, the way she molds right into her spot on my neck.

When she awakens, I gently prompt her to climb up onto my back. Although I can tell her heart's not in it, she dutifully obeys, probably thinking that I'm trying to cheer her up. I am, though not in the manner she thinks.

My heart is heavy as I land on the ground in the forest beside her village. "Get down," I tell her gently.

She slides off my neck and looks up at me questioningly. I'm sure she's wondering what's going on because I've never landed with her anywhere. I usually take her for a flight and then we go back to the cave. "Go," I tell her gently.

Her eyes widen, and she looks up at me. "What?" her voice trembles.

"Go on and take care of your sister." My chest is so tight, it's all I can do to get the words out.

Tears spring to her eyes, and her throat works as she continues to stare at me. "Go on now," I prompt her again. "She needs you."

I know I don't imagine it this time because I see it with my own eyes. She leans up and kisses my neck before she whispers, "I'll come back to you as soon as she's better."

I don't say anything. I can't. I merely turn and fly off into the sky back toward the cave with all of my treasures that suddenly mean nothing without her.

I know Macy may mean well when she says she'll come back to me, but I know in my heart that she won't because what human in her right mind would willingly choose to live the half-life Macy has been living with a dragon?

She was making the most of it, and maybe she really did come to like me and enjoy my company, but now she's back where she belongs. She can live among her own kind with her sister, her people. She can be with a man who could love her the way she deserves to be loved.

At that thought, pain floods my chest so swiftly, I can't contain it. I roar, breathing fire out across the land as I swoop and soar furiously to work out my rage.

I finally had something that gives my life meaning, and I had to let it go—against all my instincts telling me not to.

Things only get worse whenever I return to my cave because there's a white glow emanating from it, and when I land inside, I see that I'm no longer alone.

The Goddess is here. Just great.

Blaine

"Goddess, to what do I owe this pleasure?" My voice is dry, but I'm beyond the niceties. That's as good as she's going to get out of me.

My heart is tired, and I feel like my soul has been ripped away from my body. I don't care if she leaves or stays. I plan on curling up into a ball and just dying up here in this cave because what's the point in living now?

The goddess smiles at me. Her silvery hair hangs down to her feet. Despite her graying hair, her face still retains that of a youthful appearance. With full pink lips and big blue eyes, I'm sure she's beautiful, but she pales in comparison to my little treasure. Everyone does.

"You disobeyed my orders." She speaks coolly, despite her smile.

I'm disinterested in her ire. "So, destroy me."

She raises a delicate eyebrow at me. "That's not exactly why I'm here."

I don't ask her why she's here. I just look at her, beyond caring and feeling every one of my centuries. I'm too exhausted to play her little games.

She goes on as if I did ask her, though. "I am here to set you free."

I don't know what she's talking about, but it's of no consequence.

She doesn't wait for me to express any interest before she flicks her wrist.

And then I feel as if I'm falling over. The air is pushing in on me, and I'm sure that she has granted my request to destroy me because I can't breathe. I wish it would hurry up and be over it.

The intense pressure finally gives way. I blink, and when I open my eyes, I'm level with her. My eyes narrow with suspicion. Just what the hell is going on here?

I suddenly notice that I'm no longer standing on all fours. I feel different. I move my arms and am shocked to see that instead of my scaly appendages, I have human hands. I hold them up in front of my face in wonder before I gaze down over my suddenly very human body.

I'm completely naked, but I'm much too shocked by my new state to be embarrassed. Besides, I've lived my entire life without clothing as a dragon, so I'm without the shame that humans usually have about their nudity.

How can this be? How am I a human?

I look up at the goddess, my eyes wide now.

"What—?" I ask, but she laughs. The sound is like the light tinkling of bells, though not nearly as satisfying as the sound of my Macy's sweet laughter.

"So I finally have your attention?" she smiles at me in amusement.

"Why did you change me into a human?" I don't get what she's playing at.

"I didn't *change* you into a human," she tells me patiently. "You've always been a human—well, half human anyway, but you were a slave to your dragon."

I just gape at her in confusion.

"You don't remember being human because you were born with both dragon blood and human blood. However, when you were just a babe, your dragon side quickly took over your human side, smothering it within you."

"Are you telling me all this time I could have been human?"

She shakes her head. "Not quite, my child. You had to overcome your beastly urges and display more humanity than dragon, which you have just done by letting your greatest treasure go." She smiles at me sympathetically before she goes on softly with something akin to pride in her eyes. "I know what that cost you."

My heart quickens at the reminder of Macy. Now that I'm a human...

As if the goddess can read my thoughts, she tsks and wags a finger at me. "Before you go getting ahead of yourself, you must know that you will remain in your human state so long as you don't go after Macy."

A growl rumbles up out of my throat, and I don't even try to contain my frustration as I snap at my creator, "Then what's the point of all this?"

She goes on calmly, ignoring my brief outburst. "Macy said she would return to you. You must trust that she will. If she does, you will remain in your human form forever and be free to go wherever you wish, but until she does, you must stay up here on this mountaintop as you did when you were a dragon and await her."

"But—" I begin, but before I can utter a word of protest, she vanishes in a cloud of smoke.

I run my hands over my head and marvel at the tuft of hair I find there. I'm buzzing in anticipation as I go over to pick up the mirror to see my treasure.

Please come back to me. Please, my little treasure.

She's caring for her sister. My heart swells. As much as I hated to let her go, even if she never comes back to me, I know I did the right thing.

I'll content myself with watching her from afar like this, if that's what it takes.

CHAPTER

EIGHT

Macy

When I first return to the village, my sister falls into delirium. Her fever is so severe, all I can focus on is taking care of her. I sit vigil by her bedside, but when it's quiet and she sleeps, my thoughts inevitably keep drifting back to Blaine.

My heart squeezes every time I think of him. I miss him. The way his voice rumbles when he speaks softly as I lay in my spot on his neck, the way his amber eyes glow as they watch every move I make.

I remember how I told him I would go back to

him, and I meant it, but every time I look at my sister, I wonder how I can leave her again. True, she seemed to do fine on her own until she got sick, but what if she gets sick again and doesn't have anyone there to take care of her?

And even though I think Blaine wants me, he doesn't need me the way Bree does.

She's delirious for three days, during which all I can do is sit and hold her hand in between sponging off her forehead and trying to feed her sips of water and hot broth.

To fill the silence, I speak to her. I recall good memories from when our parents were alive. I tell her I'm sorry for leaving her but that I didn't have a choice. I know Bree knows that and understands, but I feel the need to tell her anyway.

And then I inevitably tell her about Blaine, smiling and crying in turns as I recount memories of my time with my dragon. I confess things to her I've never even confessed myself. As impossible as it seems, I think I'm in love with him. Even though he's a dragon and I know we could never be together the way a man and a woman are, I still love him. I desperately wish he was a man.

Even though Bree lays unresponsive as I tell her all this, it still feels good to bare my soul to someone and to face the truth that I haven't been able to face myself.

"I'm alright. You should go back to him."

I'm startled out of my thoughts by Bree's weak voice that I haven't heard since I came back to find her sick.

"Bree!" I sit up and clasp her hands between my own, overjoyed that she seems to be out of her delirium now. Tears of relief are spilling down my cheeks as I stroke her hair back from her face. "Bree! How are you feeling? Here! Take some water."

I hold the water up to her lips. She takes a few sips and then shakes her head, declining anymore. "Your dragon," she insists. "You should go back to him. You love him. And it sounds like he loves you."

I shake my head as I shush her. "Don't worry about that now. I wouldn't have even told you that if I thought you could hear me and that it would bother you."

"Doesn't bother me," she denies. Her eyes are shining as she gazes up at me. "Makes me happy. I was worried about you." Now her eyes are the ones brimming with tears. "Was afraid you were dead, and all this time you've been taken care of. You deserve to be happy, Macy."

"But you had no one to take care of you," I tell her.

Bree shakes her head. "Don't need anyone. I love you, Macy. You're my big sister, and you always will be, but it's time for you to live your own life and not worry about me. I may be young, but I've managed on my own ever since you left. Me getting sick could have happened to anyone. Don't worry about me, sister. It sounds like you may have found a rare type of happiness. Yeah, it sounds complicated." She gives my hand a little squeeze. "But you deserve the chance to chase it."

"Hush now," I tell her. "We'll talk about this more when you're all better. I'm not leaving you now, Bree."

My sister must hear the finality in my voice because she gives a brief nod and lets it go for the timeline.

Still, I can't stop smiling and marveling over how wise and grown-up my little sister suddenly sounds.

Blaine

Whereas Macy used to just use the mirror to check in on her sister, I use it obsessively. I stare at it all day to watch every move Macy makes. She takes care of her sister, vigilantly sitting by her and stroking her hair. My fingers itch with the need to see what Macy's hair and skin feel like through human hands. The ache is so real I feel it in my physical being.

My heart quickens when I hear Macy speaking to her sister about me. I think my heart will explode when I hear Macy confessing to her sister that she feels the same way about me, except she thinks our love is doomed because I'm a dragon.

Desperation washes over me. I want to scream through the mirror to her to come back, that I am no longer a dragon, that I'm a man now who can love her the way she deserves to be loved, but I can't do that.

My heart pumps into overdrive when I hear her sister pushing her to come back to me. I peer closer at the mirror, waiting with bated breath to hear Macy's response.

As fate would have it, the mirror stops working at that exact moment. I let out a roar of frustration and shake it a few times, as if that will make it come back. When it doesn't, I finally fling the mirror against the wall in fury, letting out a roar as I do so. I either have shit for luck or the goddess is putting me through another test with her evil sense of humor.

I stomp around my cave, screaming and venting my frustration with colorful curses. Of course, no one can hear me except maybe the goddess, and if she is up there, she's probably laughing her ass off.

A week goes by and then two, and there's still no sign of Macy. Dejected and forlorn, I must face the facts that she must have decided that despite her feelings, it's not worth going through the disappointment that we can never truly be together the way we want to be.

I can't really blame her. She deserves so much more. She deserves a husband, a family. My hands ball into fists at the thought of her with another man, though. It makes me want to say to hell with all of this and risk the chance of ever being with her and morphing back into my dragon form just to go get her and drag her back to my cave with me. Having her in my dragon form, just watching her and never being able to hold her as a man, is better than nothing.

But I know I can't condemn her to that fate. That's why I refrain from storming out of the cave, even though every instinct within me is telling me to go claim her as my own.

Like the goddess said, she had a choice. She could have come back to me. She chose not to. I should just be glad that we had what we had for as long as we did. By her own admission, she fell in love with me, despite me being a dragon. I can take all the memories of her with me to the grave. That's more than I ever thought I would have in my pitiful existence.

I head over to Macy's area, the bed that she never slept in, preferring to sleep in the crook of my neck. I sleep there every night where I can still smell her sweet scent. She smells like violets, though the scent is fading.

I suppose when it completely fades, I'll just fade away too.

I'll have no purpose for living anymore.

NINE

Macy

I'm huffing and puffing by the time I make it up to the mouth of the cave on my own. The journey was much more arduous on my own without the two men gripping my arms between them and practically carrying me up the slopes.

I would have been here sooner, but I stayed with my sister to make sure she was fully recovered and to meet her beau before I came up. He's a wonderful young man only a couple of years older than me, and it doesn't take a genius to see he's completely besotted with Bree and will do right by her. That much was clear when he thanked me for taking care of her and apologized for not being here himself, but he'd been away on business trying to make money to begin his life with Bree. He seems like a responsible young man with a good head on his shoulders, and I felt completely confident leaving her in his hands.

Once I saw my sister will be properly taken care of and that she's going to soon be starting a family of her own, I finally felt okay about going back up on top of the mountain—back to my dragon.

Blaine.

I know that more than a few of the townsfolk think I'm crazy. They don't know the full story between me and Blaine—not like Bree does. They probably think I escaped and that I'm off my rocker to go back, but I don't care what anyone thinks. All I care about is getting back to Blaine.

My heart skips a beat as I near the mouth of the cave. I can't wait to see him again.

When I breach the opening, I still, my heart immediately falling when I don't see my dragon inside. He's not here because if he was, I would have spotted him immediately. He's so huge he takes up nearly the entire cave.

"Blaine," I whisper mournfully.

I jump when I hear shuffling from the back corner of the cave. My eyes cut over to my makeshift bed area, my heart pinging with memories of Blaine bringing me all the fabrics to make it with.

A man emerges from it, and I'm suddenly angry as hell that someone would invade what in my mind is still me and Blaine's personal space. "How dare you!" I seethe. "You shouldn't be squatting in here. This cave belongs to someone."

The man doesn't wince at my harsh tone, nor does he speak. Instead, he simply stands in the shadows and stares at me. Even though I can't see his eyes, I feel them boring into me so intensely goosebumps erupt across my flesh.

I can't make out all his features, only that he's tall and bulky.

He lets out a sigh, a sigh that sounds somehow familiar. Then he steps into the light, and I gasp. He has thick auburn hair that waves back from his face. His jawline is strong, and his chest is bare since he's only wearing a pair of breeches. And sweet goddess at all the muscles there. The man looks like he was sculpted from the rock formations of the mountain itself, but none of that is what causes my gasp or catches my eye.

No, what catches my attention the most is his eyes. They're eerily familiar, a glowing amber that I've only ever seen once before. It can't...it can't be...

Then, I get a tingling sense of déjà vu as I realize this is what Blaine looked like in my dreams.

"Blaine?" I whisper incredulously, hopefully.

"Macy." His voice comes out as a law rasp, but I instantly recognize it as that of my dragon.

"Blaine!" I say his name again as I run over to him and then stop just short of him shyly.

His nostrils flare, and he reaches out a trembling hand to me tentatively. "Are you really here?" he whispers. "Have you come back to me?"

I'm shaking my head, unable to believe this is real, wondering if I'm dreaming. "How can this be? You're a dragon."

He gives me a crooked grin. "Not anymore. Thanks to you."

"Me?" I blink incredulously.

Blaine nods. "Apparently, you unlocked my humanity. When I set you free, I performed my first selfless act, and it was enough for the goddess to set free the man inside me."

"So, you're not a dragon anymore?"

He shrugs. "I suppose a part of me will always be a beast, but that part is now overruled by the man you brought out of me." His eyes become pained as he tells me, "I watched you every day when you were gone—until the damned mirror stopped working, that is."

My breath hitches at the knowledge. Of course! The mirror that I used to watch my sister with. How could I have forgotten it? I blush at the thought of Blaine watching me and what all he might have heard and saw. But at some point, he said the mirror stopped working, so that explains why he didn't know I was coming.

"Why did you come back?" he asks me, his voice husky.

My cheeks turn pink as I look him straight in the eye and tell him, "If you've been watching me, then don't you already know?"

He takes a step toward me before his voice drops a note. He cups my cheek before he whispers, his voice a low caress, "Yes, my love, but I want to hear it directly from your lips."

"You first," I whisper.

His eyes light with humor before he tells me huskily, "I love you, Macy."

My heart gallops away in my chest. Joy explodes deep inside me. The words come tumbling from me unrestrained, "I love you too, Blaine. I loved you even when you were a dragon."

"I know," he croons to me, his thumb stroking tenderly over my cheek.

"I would have come back even if you were still a dragon," I tell him. "In fact, I did. I thought you were a dragon, and I came back."

"I know," he reassures me again. "That's part of how I know your love is so true."

We stare at each other for a moment. He looks so different in his human form, and yet he's the same. His eyes are the same, and in his auburn hair, I can almost see his red scales that deepened into that dark purple that I loved on him as a dragon. He has the same mouth, the same expressions. He's still *my* Blaine.

"So now what?" I whisper when he keeps staring at me.

His eyes darken. "Now, I love you the way a man loves a woman," he tells me before he cups my face in his hands. His eyes blaze down into mine as he lowers his head slowly to my lips.

When his lips touch mine, I feel like I'm finally home.

CHAPTER
TEN

Blaine

She came back to me. Macy. My little treasure.

She tastes as sweet as she looks, like pure-spun sugar and honey. I can't get enough of her. The gentle press of her lips underneath mine is enough to send fire licking throughout my veins. I deepen the kiss, slipping my tongue inside the wet cave of her mouth where her sweetness is only amplified tenfold.

I fist my fingers through her silken locks, marveling at the feel of them. Of course, I felt them on my scales before, but feeling them with human hands is unlike anything I could have ever imagined.

Her skin is petal soft underneath my fingertips as I run them along the creamy column of her flesh and over her bare shoulder. "You're wearing the same dress you wore the day you were sacrificed to me," I note.

She smiles up at me shyly. "I remember you liked it."

"I did." I tell her approvingly. "I still do. You look beautiful in it."

She runs her fingers over my bare chest, and I can't contain the shiver that passes through me at the sensation. It has my cock lengthening and hardening in my breeches. She feels it too if her wide eyes and suddenly parted lips are any indication.

She surprises me when she takes the lead and aggressively presses her lips back against mine. More blood rushes to my aching staff as she flutters her lips over mine and presses her body into mine until her breasts and stomach are pressed flush against me. "Take me, Blaine," she whispers against my lips, "Make me yours in every way."

Even though her words fill me with a rush of lust so potent, it almost knocks me over, I hold back. I pull back from her long enough to grin down at her. "I thought you said I wasn't going to split you apart with my big dragon dick."

Macy laughs and then burrows her face in the crook of my neck. I sigh with contentment at the feeling of her head in my neck right where she belongs. She might not can spoon her whole body into my neck anymore, but having her face there is enough. If anything, it feels even better because now I can wrap my arms around her as she does it.

"You're right," she finally concedes as she pulls back from me. "We're moving too fast. We should slow—"

I don't give her a chance to finish that sentence before I crash my lips on to hers, kissing her voraciously and humping my thickness against her through our clothing, letting her know in no uncertain terms just how much I want her. "I was just teasing you. There's no way I'm letting you go now, my little treasure. You're going to be mine in every way before the night is over."

I kiss her again, and she whimpers into my mouth. I feel that whimper in my soul. It ignites a fire deep in my belly that only she'll be able to quench.

When I slide her dress off her shoulders, she

stills me with a hand on my chest. "Wait Blaine, I've never..." She bites her lips, and my chest warms with satisfaction.

I already knew she was a virgin, but hearing her confirm it to me again and seeing how suddenly shy she is fills me with a rush of tenderness for her. "I know, my love. I've never done this before, either."

Her eyes widen. "As a dragon, or as a man?"

"Both, I tell her honestly. "I'm a virgin too, so we'll learn together."

She places a soft kiss on my chest, and I don't know why, but that detonates something inside me. Suddenly, I'm desperate to be inside her. I *need* to be one with her.

I slide her dress down her until it falls over her hips and pools at her feet. Then, I quickly shuck off my own clothing.

She gasps when my swollen length bobs free and looks up at me with worry in her eyes.

"Shh," I soothe her. "I promise it'll fit. You were made for me, and I'll be gentle. We can go as slow as you want. I won't do anything you don't want me to do."

She nods and steps forward in silent offering. I groan. It's an offering I can't turn down.

I scoop her into my arms and carry her over to her bed. I lay her gently on it and then kiss on over her body, worshiping her like the treasure she is. I pause several times just to stare at her and drink in the lovely vision she makes. She's so sweet, especially when I reach the nectar between her legs.

I almost come on the spot at the taste of her. How does she taste just as sweet there as she does in her mouth? "Like sugar and honey," I rasp against her wet folds.

She moans when I find the bud of her pleasure and lick and suck on it. I'm holding her open with a hand on each of her thighs, and I can feel them trembling beneath my hands.

And when I increase the suction on that little bud, batting it with my tongue, she shivers and moans underneath me. I take my cues from her body, following her sighs and moans like they're a roadmap to her pleasure.

Finally, she tenses up and screams my name before fisting her fingers into my hair and pulling. The bite is painful, but I barely feel it. I'm too gone in my own euphoric rush of feeling her fall apart underneath me. Her muscles are spasming and convulsing, and I can't help sticking the tip of a finger in her wet hole to feel it. I imagine what it's going to feel like doing that on my swollen length and curse as my need grows stronger than ever. "Macy, are you ready for me, my love?"

She nods her head up at me deliriously. "Yes, I need you, Blaine. Now!"

I line myself up with her hole and begin pushing gently into her, feeling her flesh stretch impossibly around me. I'm so thick, and she's so tiny, the fit snug. It's so snug that my eyes roll back in my head.

I grit my teeth, fighting for control. I don't want to ejaculate too soon. I want to make this last. I want to give her another orgasm—this time on my cock.

My little Macy surprises me once again when she places her hands on my ass and pulls me down into her while thrusting her hips upward.

She lets out a keening sound, and I feel myself pop through the barrier of her innocence. I let out a long curse as my entire body trembles at the sudden feeling of being completely engulfed inside her hot, wet channel. My groin is pressed right up against hers, and it's taking everything in me to not spill inside her right now.

I gather her to my chest, holding her close in my arms, and plant kisses all over her face as I rain praises down upon her. "So beautiful. Made for me. My little treasure. You're mine now. You know that? Mine forever."

"Yes, I'm yours," she agrees with me as she kisses me back.

I'm filled with so much emotion I can hardly contain it all, but then my body takes over, and I can no longer sit still. "I have to move, Macy."

"Yes," she agrees with me as she lifts her hips up to me in offering. The way this precious girl keeps offering herself to me is going to be my undoing. I feel myself sliding inside her at the movement and let out a guttural groan of my own before I pull my hips back and stroke in and out of her—slowly at first and then picking up momentum until I'm pulling nearly all the way out and slamming back into her.

"Yes, yes!" she's chanting.

"Mine, mine, mine!" I'm chanting.

"Blaine!" She finally screams my name, and I feel her fluttering around me.

That's all it takes to set me off. "Yes! I'm there too, my love. Come with me, Macy!"

And she does—hard. Her muscles contract around me more forcefully than they did on my tongue. The sensation of her milking me sends me toppling over the edge. My release rushes up from my stalk. I hold myself deep as I moan and spill myself into her womb.

We're both sweating and breathing heavily, holding each other tightly. By the time we float back down to earth, I kiss Macy's forehead lovingly. She smiles up at me dreamily. "You know, I wanted to kill that oracle for choosing me to be sacrificed to you," he notes with a little smile, "but now I guess I should thank her."

"I'm the one who should thank her," I tell her before I place an affectionate kiss on her nose.

"Because you got your humanity back?" Macy smiles at me knowingly.

I shake my head. "No, because she gave me *you*. My greatest treasure."

Macy's smile brightens up the entire cave, charming my once-stony heart.

Hey there, you gorgeous reading machine!

First of all, THANK YOU for spending your precious time with my characters and letting me take up space in your brain for a while. You could've been doing literally anything else—like scrolling social media or alphabetizing your spice rack—but instead, you chose this. And I love you for it.

Now, let me let you in on a little secret: I'm basically the romance writing equivalent of a shapeshifter. One author, multiple personalities. Here are the pen names I write under:

- Emma Bray — steamy contemporary romance that's all heart eyes and heat
- Kenzie Skye — spicy romantasy and paranormal goodness—magic, monsters, and all the feels
- DAHLIA — downright filthy, dirty, naughty erotic romance (It's okay if you like it. I won't tell. 😏)
- E.B. Fox — dark, broody, edge-of-your-seat romance for when you want to walk on the wild side

Craving more? Head to www.spicy-romance.com and sign up for my newsletter. As a thank-you, you'll get a free book you can't find anywhere else. (Check out this preview to get a sample of it.)

And I promise, cross my heart and swear on

my sexiest plot twist: I will NEVER spam you. Only juicy updates, exclusive goodies, and sneak peeks that'll leave you begging for more.

Stay spicy, stay amazing, and keep chasing those happily ever afters (or wickedly dark ones— no judgment).

Big hugs and even bigger love,

The romance writing shapeshifter

P.S. Did I mention you're awesome? Because you are. 

P.S.S. Here are some super handy-dandy lists where you can find all of my books:

- books2read.com/rl/emmabray
- books2read.com/rl/kenzieskye
- books2read.com/rl/dahlia
- books2read.com/rl/ebfox

Keep reading for an excerpt from the next Steamy Shifter Romance: Taken by the Tiger King.

TAKEN BY THE TIGER KING

I prowl along the city streets, my senses on high alert—as ever. I know what I'm looking for, but I don't know how I'll know when I find it. All I know is that I will *know*. And I know that doesn't make much sense, but that's the way of our mating.

To the disappointment of many of the females in our streak, none of them call to me as my mate, and tiger streaks aren't the same as lion prides. Whereas if a lion doesn't find his fated mate in his pride, he will still marry within his pride, settling for less just to keep the bloodline pure, that's not the way of us tigers. We know that not only will marrying your true fated mate make you as strong as you can be, but it will lead to a happier tiger who will perform better for the entire streak. It not only benefits the tiger in question, but the streak as a whole, and since I am the tiger king, it's doubly important for me to find my fated mate rather than settling. I'm not only seeking her for my own happiness, but for the well-being of my entire streak.

Still, it's a bitch and a pain in my ass that I couldn't have been fated to one of the females in my streak. It certainly would have made this a lot easier. But, of course, as fate would have it, I have yet to stumble across my mate, so I'm out here looking for her.

It's unlikely I'll find her at work since most of the businesses my streak runs are employed almost exclusively by members of our streak. The lions might have their hands in oil and all the transportation businesses, but us tigers are in control of most of the agricultural ones. I happen to be the CEO of the biggest agricultural importing and exporting business in the city.

I snarl when I walk past the lion king's high rise. The fuckers keep charging so much for gas prices, and it's making it more difficult for my business to turn a profit. It's also making it diffi-cult for the entire population because everybody needs food, and that's what my business supplies.

The fucking lions are the supposed kings of the jungle. They're supposed to look out for everyone, but they're nothing but a bunch of cutthroats looking to gouge anyone any way they can. They essentially fuck the entire world up the ass.

I continue to walk along the street amongst all the humans and other shifters going about their day-to-day work. Of course, the humans know about us shifters. They know the lions are in charge of the oil and the tigers are in charge of agriculture and that the wolves just don't give a fuck and like to stay off in the mountains to themselves. Wolves have always been selfish creatures. The bears are over the fishing industry and help the humans somewhat.

Regardless, there's one thing all of us shifters have in common. We have designated reservations where we do our shifting. When we're around humans and within city limits, we're to remain in our human form at all times. That is the one big law among our kind concerning the humans. While the humans know there are shifters among them, they can't tell just by looking at us what we are, and it just stresses so many of them to see one of us shift in front of them. Plus, it's also detrimental to their safety oftentimes, so that's why the council over the shifters put the law in place in the first place. It's much more difficult to control our animalistic natures when we're in our animal forms, and that oftentimes leads to humans getting hurt. They're such delicate creatures, sensitive and in need of our care and protection, whether or not they realize it.

I scowl, my irritation rising to new heights as I realize my search has been fruitless. It could take me years to find my mate at this rate, and I'm impatient enough as it is. I can't focus on properly ruling my streak with this insatiable need inside me. I'm a tiger in his prime, and my biological clock is screaming at me to take my mate. And I would gladly do so if only I could find her.

I grunt as someone bumps into me—hard. But the impact doesn't hurt me at all or barely budge me. Still, it's enough to garner my attention, and my hands shoot out to steady the tiny female in front of me before she topples to the ground. A reprimand about how she should watch where she's going is on the tip of my tongue. I'm usually not so rude, but she caught me in a bad moment.

My sharp words die on my tongue, though, when her eyelashes flutter up to me. I'm assaulted by her big blue eyes. They're a crystal-clear blue, the blue of a cloudless sky on a summer day. My chest tightens as they hold me captive. I'm unable to tear my gaze from their shining depths.

My breathing becomes ragged as all the neurons in my brain fire. My blood rushes through my veins, hot and heavy. I'm hyper-aware of her bare shoulders underneath my fingertips where I'm still gripping her. The feeling of her skin underneath mine sends electricity shooting through my palms and up my arms.

Her puffy pink lips fall open in a little gasp, and I finally tear my eyes away from her blue orbs long enough to note that her hair is a fiery red. It's a beautiful mane of curls that cascades down her back in luxurious waves. She looks like one of those pretty porcelain dolls women collect. Her skin is creamy and silky and smooth. I can tell she's not wearing any makeup, yet she's flawless. She looks too flawless to be real.

She smells young and innocent and ripe, like fresh berries. She's undoubtedly a virgin and young. So very young. Dainty. Pretty. Gorgeous. There aren't enough adjectives to describe what she is, what she makes me feel.

I already know she's my mate before a word

comes out of her mouth, so all the other points are moot. Still, I ask her anyway, "How old are you?"

Her pretty brow furrows, and she looks up at me in confusion. "What?" Her voice is so soft and pretty, like a light tinkling of bells, and fuck if it doesn't make my cock hard.

"Are you eighteen?" I ask her, my voice coming out more roughly than I intend.

She blinks at me obviously, taken aback before she bristles. "No."

My heart plummets. Fuck, how can she be my mate if she's not even of legal age...

"I'm nineteen."

Relief crashes through me. Humans claim to understand a bit of our mating rituals, but they have their own laws. I don't need to be making trouble with them by getting involved with a minor, so thank fuck, my mate is legal. She's barely legal, but legal.

I inhale a deep breath, trying to get a deeper read on her scent. I don't smell any shifter in her at all. She's pure human, and while it's not unheard of for shifters to have a human mate, it's rare for someone higher in the hierarchy like me. A tiger king almost always has a shifter mate, someone who understands the streak's ways and can help him with his leadership.

My little mate is certainly no tigress, but there's no helping it. Every atom in my body is screaming at me she's the one, and I'm helpless to fight this even if I wanted to. Which I don't.

My eyes greedily drink her in. My mate is beautiful. She's everything I could have ever wanted and more. I never imagined one so perfect. The way I'm staring at her must start to freak her out because she pulls against my hold and apologizes weakly, "Yeah, I'm sorry I bumped into you. I'm late for work—"

She lets out a little oomph as I suddenly pick her up and fling her over my shoulder caveman style. I don't give a fuck that we're in the middle of a busy street. I dare anyone to try to stop me from taking my mate.

She screeches, "Put me down!" She tries to kick, but I band my arm around her legs and hold her little dress down so that no other males get a flash of the sweet ass that is mine. The scent of her pussy drifts over to my nostrils, and I inhale deeply, precum leaking from the tip of my cock in response.

I begin stalking down the street with her. A

few humans stop and stare, but none dare challenge me. I can tell who the shifters are already because one glance at us and they look hurriedly away, knowing better than to get involved in the tiger king's claiming of his mate. They know very well what's going on.

My mate keeps kicking and screaming as I carry her into my building and go straight for the elevator. Only when we're locked inside do I set her on her feet and stare down at her intently, taking in the beautiful flush to her cheeks and the way her blue eyes are flashing with anger rather than fear.

"What's your name?" I demand, needing to know what to call my mate. I can't keep referring to her as "mate." That, and I'm genuinely interested in knowing what my mate's name is. I want to know everything about her.

Instead of answering me, she soundly slaps me across the cheek.

I grin as I feel the sting.

Oh yes, she will make a fine tiger queen.

Keep reading Taken by the Tiger King here: https://books2read.com/takenbythetigerking

SEX AND CANDY - EXCLUSIVE FREEBIE

She's too sweet to resist. And she's mine. All mine.

Ace

Three things are for sure:

One: She's the most stunning little thing I've ever laid eyes on.

Two: She doesn't belong on that stage, shaking it for men who don't deserve to breathe her air.

Three: She's already mine—even if she doesn't know it yet.

And I don't care what I have to do to prove it.

Candy

Only two things in life are for sure:

One: Nothing in life comes without a price.

Two: Men only ever want one thing.

But Ace? He's not like the others. He's dangerous, possessive, and makes promises I've never heard before. I should run... but every instinct in me tells me to stay.

Sex and Candy is a *steamy-as-sin* romance featuring an obsessive billionaire alpha who will do anything—*anything*—to claim his woman. He's intense, over-the-top, and completely irresistible. Protective? Yes. Possessive? Hell yes. HEA? Always.

Keep reading for a preview of Sex and Candy:

. . .

I take a sip of the subpar whiskey in front of me and grimace at the taste as I glance down at my Rolex. Fucker's late.

I drum my fingers on the table in irritation, keenly reminded of why I never let anyone pick meeting locations. You never know what kind of seedy joint they're going to want to meet up in or if they'll even show up at all.

I knew better than to let MacHay dictate the terms of this meeting, but I went against my better instincts and did it anyway. Simply because the man has proven so difficult to get in touch with. I'm regretting ever shaking his hand in the first place, and if I wasn't beholden to hold up my end of the bargain, I'd say fuck it and bail on this here and now.

Oh, well. You live and learn, right?

I'm tempted to do it anyway and am actually moving to slip out of my booth when the stage lights up and a hush falls over the audience.

I don't know what causes me to pause and sit back down. It's probably just going to be another subpar dancer like all the other ones that have been staggering around on the stage all night.

Maybe it's the pregnant pause of anticipation that seems to fall over the entire room.

I don't know.

But when the tiniest little angel I've ever seen steps on stage, time itself seems to stop.

Her skin glows ivory under the stage light. She has on a lacy white number, some sort of bustier, lacy panties, and white stockings. The look is topped off with fire engine red heels that match the paint on her lips. Long lashes frame light brown eyes that look too big and luminous for her little heart-shaped face. Long blonde hair like spun gold falls in glorious waves all the way down to an impossibly tiny waist that I know I could cup in my two hands. My breath catches in my throat. My god, she looks like a porcelain doll come to life.

But what most arrests me is the look in her eyes. For a split second when she first steps out on stage, her wide eyes are soulfully sad, so much so that they seem to take my breath away.

They seem to mirror all the tragedy in the world in their depths.

But then it's gone in the blink of an eye as she smiles, a dazzling, heart-wrenching smile that makes me instantly jealous. I'm irrationally upset that's she's gracing this roomful of men with that smile—that smile that I suddenly know deep down in my soul is meant to be only mine.

Mine.

Sultry music begins to play, and she begins to dance, gently swaying her hips as she flirts with the strip pole.

I'm gripping the edge of the table so tightly I'm surprised the wood doesn't break underneath my palms. I swear to God if one piece of clothing comes off her body I won't be able to stop myself from rushing up on that stage and covering her from prying eyes.

I'm aware that my reaction is insane. I don't know anything about this girl, but I can't stop the surge of possessive protectiveness that rages inside me at the thought of all these men seeing her so scantily clad like this.

What the fuck is she doing? Doesn't she know she's an angel? Doesn't she know she doesn't belong in here with all these devils?

I grit my teeth when she suddenly flings herself on the pole and begins to do a series of complicated flips and turns. The men roar and whistle and cheer, and I'd bet my last million half the fuckers in this place have a boner right now imagining her little body writhing on their laps like she is on that pole.

The thought fills me with murderous rage.

I'm so distracted by it that I don't even notice when MacHay finally takes his seat across from me until he chuckles and comments, "It's your first time witnessing the wonder that is Candy, huh?"

"What?" I bark at him, never tearing my eyes away from the beauty up on the stage. I feel like I won't be able to rest until her set is over and she's safely back behind that stage curtain where she belongs out of sight of lascivious male eyes.

He juts his chin out at the stage. "Candy. She's the feature dancer here." I spare a sideways glance at him out of the corner of my eye. He takes a sip of his drink and motions toward the stage with it, "And you can see why. Not only is she the prettiest one out of the bunch, but she's also the youngest and the one with the most skill. Consequently, she's the one Dan hoards to himself like the finest treasure. You can pay for a little extra with the other dancers, if you know what I mean, but Dan won't let anyone near Candy for no amount of money."

I frown, though I can't help feeling some sort of relief at the thought that Candy isn't being prostituted out. I can barely stomach the thought of all these men's eyes on her, much less their hands.

"So," MacHay rubs his hands together eagerly as Candy's show ends and she leaves the stage. I notice how she doesn't scramble to pick up any of the money thrown on the stage for her like all the dancers before her did. She walks coolly off the stage without even a backward glance at all the men she now holds in her thrall. "You really to get down to business?" MacHay interrupts my thoughts.

I scowl at him. The fucker keeps me waiting all the time, and then he shows up and expects me to cater to him. He can fucking wait now.

I level him with a cool stare before I stand from the booth and pull out my phone. "I have something to attend to first. If you want to see any part of this partnership go forward, you'll be sitting right here waiting for me when I get back."

He frowns and looks like he wants to say something, but one look at my tight jawline and he obviously thinks better of it, giving a curt nod of understanding instead. Yeah, he knows he fucked up.

I step out of earshot and call my head of security.

"Yeah, James? Get me everything you can on a dancer at the club on Sixth. Pronto. I want everything within the next thirty minutes. Goes by the name of Candy..."

Get your exclusive copy of Sex and Candy by signing up for my newsletter here: www.spicy-romance.com.